Robin Hood's Day

JOSEPHINE FEENEY

ILLUSTRATED BY
KATE SHEPPARD

**WALKER
BOOKS**

In memory of Lillian "Lila" Tebbutt,
a truly inspirational person
J. F.

For Carl, with love
K. S.

First published 2007 by Walker Books Ltd
87 Vauxhall Walk, London SE11 5HJ

2 4 6 8 10 9 7 5 3 1

Text © 2007 Josephine Feeney
Illustrations © 2007 Kate Sheppard

The right of Josephine Feeney and Kate Sheppard to be identified as author
and illustrator respectively of this work has been asserted by them in
accordance with the Copyright, Designs and Patents Act 1988

This book has been typeset in Bembo Educational
and Tree-Boxelder

Printed and bound in Great Britain by
Creative Print and Design (Wales), Ebbw Vale

British Library Cataloguing in Publication Data:
a catalogue record for this book is available from the British Library

ISBN 978-1-4063-0640-8

www.walkerbooks.co.uk

Jimmy
5

Patchy Pat
25

Chelsea
45

Jimmy

On Friday, when Mrs Khan had finally got us sitting quietly on the carpet, she read us a story. It was about Robin Hood, a brave and kind man who'd had lots of adventures with his Merry Men, escaping from a wicked king. It was so exciting! When Mrs Khan finished reading, she said, "Jimmy, it's your turn to have Patchy Pat for the weekend."

7

"Yes!" I said.
I was very happy.
I had been waiting
to take Patchy Pat
home for ages.
Our teacher,
Mrs Khan,
knitted him for
us a long time ago –
and she is so clever
that if Patchy gets
a little hole she knits
another patch to cover it. That's why
he's called Patchy.

Today he looked even better. He was
wearing a new Robin Hood outfit.

8

"Now make sure you take good care of him," Mrs Khan said very seriously. "And on Monday morning you can tell us all about the adventures you've had with Patchy Pat."

Chelsea and Dad were pleased
to meet Patchy at home time.

"We'll have to think of
something really, really
exciting to do this
weekend," I told them.

Dad said, "Tell you what, Jimmy. How would you like to go on a train journey with Patchy Pat?" "Yes please, Dad," I said.

"Can I come too?" Chelsea asked. "Course you can, silly!" I said.

11

On Saturday morning we left the house very early. We caught the bus at the top of our street. I showed Patchy Pat the view from the window.

At the train station Dad bought our
train tickets, a newspaper, a colouring
book, some crayons and a notebook.
He said, "You can write down
everything you and
Patchy Pat see today.
Mrs Khan will be
very pleased
with that."

On the train we found seats next to the window, with a table to sit at. Dad took out his paper and me and Chelsea took out our things. I opened my notebook and chewed the end of my pencil to help me think about what to write. I asked, "How do you spell 'adventure'?"

"A–D–V–E–N–T–U–R–E," Dad replied, smiling.

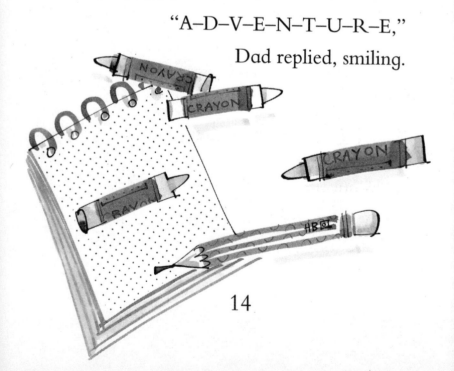

"What shall I write now?" I asked.

"Write down everything you can see
out the window."

The train began to move slowly out
of the station, creeping past the black
brick walls, then the wooden fences,

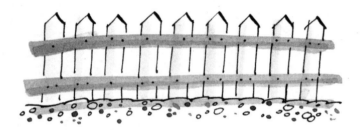

the shops, the car park, the hospital,
the school and the sports centre.

"How do you spell 'hospital', Dad?"

"Don't worry about spelling, Jimmy. Just write it the way you think it might be spelt."

"I can spell it," said Chelsea.

"I bet Patchy Pat isn't very good at spelling," I said.

The train left all the big buildings
behind and began to go past the backs
of people's houses. I could see
swings and slides and rabbit
hutches. Then we moved
out into the
countryside.
In my book
I wrote:

This is what
Patchy Pat can see:

trees
trees
lots of trees
wires
birds
trees

"It's just trees out the window, Dad," I said.

"Why don't you have another look, Jimmy. There are some hedges and fields and – look! Over there, some cows. And in the next field, some sheep and horses."

"How do you spell 'hedges', Dad?" I asked.

"H–E–J–E–S," Chelsea spelt.

In my book I wrote:

trees
hejes
cows

Then I said, "Dad, what do you
call those stripy black-and-white birds?"

"Magpies,"
Dad said.
"How do
you spell—?"

TRAIN Co.

"Don't worry about writing any more, Jimmy," Dad said. "Just sit and look out of the window and enjoy the train trip. You can tell Mrs Khan about it on Monday."

So I just looked. But
looking made me tired and
I fell asleep. When I opened my
eyes, everyone was standing up
and taking down their bags and
coats from the shelves above.
"We're here, Jimmy,"
Dad said. "We're in
Nottingham!"

Nottingham! That was where Robin Hood had lived! I put Patchy Pat and my notebook in my rucksack and me, Chelsea and Dad climbed off the train.

Patchy Pat

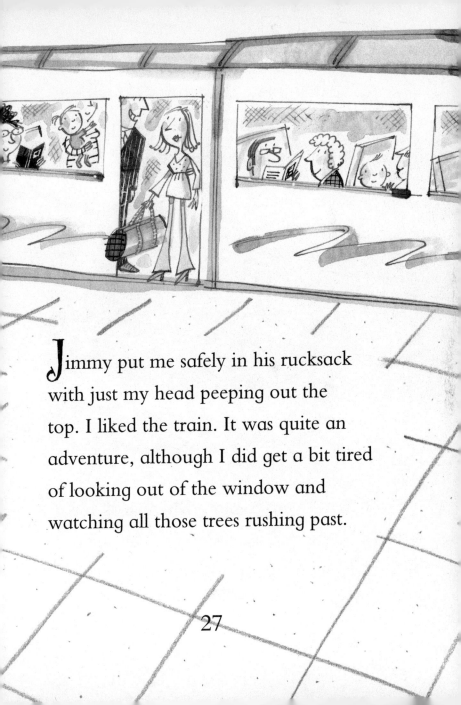

Jimmy put me safely in his rucksack
with just my head peeping out the
top. I liked the train. It was quite an
adventure, although I did get a bit tired
of looking out of the window and
watching all those trees rushing past.

I've had a few adventures in my time.
Well, you do when you live in a
different house nearly every day!

There was the night Millie took me
to her swimming lesson and left me in
the pool. I was wet through.

I had to lie on Millie's hall radiator all night. The next day, Mrs Khan said I wasn't well enough to go to anyone's house.

Delaney took me to her dancing class and left me on top of the piano for hours…

Meanwhile, she went to the library and the café and the shoe shop and only remembered me when she was on the bus back from town!

30

On Monday Delaney didn't tell
Mrs Khan about forgetting me.
She stood up and said sweetly,
"I took Patchy Pat to my dancing
class and then we went to the library
and Kate's Café and then he helped
me choose some new shoes."

You little
storyteller!
I thought to
myself, but
I didn't say
anything.

The best
adventure I had
was with Prakash.
He took me to the park
and we played in the woods.
He put me on a really high branch
and made me a lookout. He told me
to shout when Amrit crept up the hill.
It was great.

We spotted
Amrit and
jumped out and
frightened him.
"Boo!"

I've had lots of other adventures, but that day in Nottingham wasn't like any of the others. I was so excited as we walked towards Maid Marian Way.

MAID MARIAN WAY

Maid Marian! Named after Robin Hood's girlfriend, because Robin Hood came from Nottingham, Jimmy said.

Jimmy talked to me as we walked along. He calls me "Patchy", which is a nice nickname. Jimmy's dad said we should go to the café first, because he could do with a cup of coffee.

Chelsea said, "Race you to the café, Jimmy and Patchy!" She won. Jimmy and Chelsea chose big cakes. Then they sat down and Jimmy put his rucksack on the floor next to our table.

I didn't like being on the floor so far away from Jimmy. Suddenly, a big baby from the family on the next table crawled across and spotted me from behind. She pulled at my hair and dribbled over my new outfit.

37

Jimmy and Chelsea were too busy
eating their cakes to notice that I was
in *terrible danger*! The baby pulled and
pulled at my hair until I popped out of
Jimmy's rucksack. She put me under
her fist and dragged me along
the floor as she crawled
back to her mummy.

I tried to shout, to get Jimmy's
attention. I looked over at him
as the baby pulled at my Robin
Hood clothes, but he didn't
notice. Jimmy finished
his cake and wiped his
hands. He stood up and
put his rucksack on his back.

Jimmy didn't check to see if I
was still peeping out the top. His
dad said, "Come on then, let's go."
Then they walked out of the café.
Without me!

What shall I do now? I thought. When Millie left me in the swimming pool and Delaney left me on top of the piano, I knew that I was just a few minutes away from being rescued. But here, in the Robin Hood café, I was a long train journey away from safety.

What would Mrs Khan say on Monday when Jimmy told her he had left me in Nottingham?

Would I ever see Mrs Khan again?

"Come to Mummy," a voice said.
A lady leant over and picked up the
baby. "Oh, look! Somebody's left their
cuddly toy," she said.

What a cheek! I'm not a cuddly toy.
I'm Mrs Khan's Patchy Pat, if you
don't mind!

The lady looked at me. She had kind,
gentle eyes. "I'll put you over here,
next to the trays, where
you can be seen."

I sat watching people come in for lunch and waited for Jimmy to return. I hoped and hoped and hoped that he and his family would come in for something to eat. He must! I thought to myself. If there's one thing I've learned on my adventures, it's this: children are always looking for something to eat.

Chelsea

I love big sticky cakes. I like it
when the shiny, sugary bit touches the
top of my cheek. Dad knows how much
I like them and he let me have a huge
one all to myself at the Robin Hood
café. "Keep us going until lunchtime,"
he said.

We went in the lift up to the Robin Hood centre. Dad paid for us to go in, then a man dressed as an outlaw took us to the costume room.

I put on a long dress. I felt like
a princess. Jimmy dressed up as Robin
Hood, just like Patchy Pat. We all
looked great. When we were ready
we walked up the stairs with the man.

At the top of the stairs was
a little carriage and we sat in it.
The man lifted a bar down onto
our laps and we moved along into
a dark tunnel, like on a funfair ride.
"I'm scared, Dad," Jimmy whispered.
"You'll be all right," I replied, even
though I felt a tiny bit frightened too.

A few seconds later, the tunnel opened up into a small village. There were little houses and people sitting around a camp fire. We could smell the wood smoke even though it wasn't real, just pretend. Then I realized it was Robin Hood and his Merry Men! I was so excited.

The carriage moved along the cable into another tunnel and then out again, beside a castle. We could see the evil King John leaning out of one of the narrow windows. He was waving his fist at us in a very wicked way.

Eventually we reached the end of the ride and the man was there to meet us. He undid our safety belts and said, "Follow me." We walked behind him until we got to a big wooden door. The man opened it. "This is Sherwood Forest," he announced. "And in a minute, if we're quiet,

we'll see Robin Hood and his Merry Men. They're going to ask for your help."

Jimmy said,
"Dad, I need
the toilet."
Dad was
a bit cross.

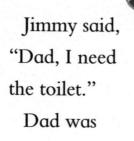

So was I.

"Why didn't you go
before we came in?"
"I didn't need to go then."
"You should have gone
anyway," I said.

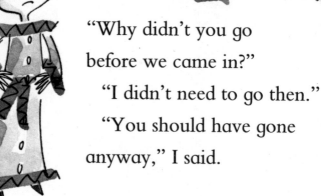

54

We walked out of the pretend Sherwood Forest and back to the toilets. "Can I bring Patchy up to the forest?" Jimmy asked.

"I'll get him for you," I said. Dad says I'm good at getting things. I ran to where we'd left our coats and bags, almost tripping over my Maid Marian dress. I found Jimmy's rucksack and opened it. Patchy wasn't there. I looked in the front pocket. He wasn't there.

Maybe Jimmy
had left him
in *my* bag.
I checked.
No, he wasn't
there either.

"Come on, Chelsea!"
Dad called.

I rushed out
to where Dad
and Jimmy were
waiting. "Patchy's
missing!" I told them.
"Are you sure?" Dad said.
"Yes, I've checked
in all the bags."

"Oh, no!" Jimmy cried.
"I've lost him! What will
Mrs Khan say? Nobody
has ever lost Patchy Pat."
"Poor Patchy," I said.
Jimmy started to cry.

"Don't worry, Jimmy," Dad said. "We'll look for him. Now, when do you remember seeing him last?"

Jimmy cried and cried. "At the ... station ... I think. I checked he was in my ... bag before we got off the train."

"Right," Dad said. "We'll retrace our steps back to the station. I'm sure we'll find Patchy on the way."

We left the Robin Hood centre and walked along Maid Marian Way, back towards the station. This is what we do when we've lost one of our gloves. We walk along and look at the pavement and sometimes we see a bright yellow or a blue spot in the distance. We run towards it and there is our glove.

But we couldn't see any bright spots. At the station we went to Lost Property, but they hadn't found Patchy.

We walked back to the Robin Hood centre and looked along every wall and hedge. Still no sign of Patchy Pat.

"What am I going … to do?" Jimmy said. His face was red with crying. "I've lost Patchy and he's all alone."

"Let's have some lunch. That will make us feel better," Dad said.

"I'm not hungry," Jimmy said. I wasn't either – I was so worried about Patchy Pat.

But Dad took us back to the Robin Hood café anyway. Jimmy went to get a tray. And guess who was sitting on a ledge near the trays?

"Patchy!"
Jimmy shouted.

He rushed over and took Patchy Pat from the ledge. "Patchy, I've found you!" Jimmy was so happy, he did a sort of dance with delight.

"I know," I said. "Let's take it in turns to carry Patchy Pat."

"Good idea," Jimmy said.

So we did, and me and Dad and
Jimmy and Patchy Pat had a great day
in Nottingham with Robin Hood and
Maid Marian.

On the way home, we all fell asleep
on the train.